FOR TILDEN AND IDA
MAY YOU ALWAYS CREATE MAGIC
WORLDS USING WHATEVER YOU HAVE.

NOT ONLY BOOKS BUT COPIES OF BOOKS
HAVE THEIR FATES.
                                    —WALTER BENJAMIN

NOTE TO THE READER/
USER:
SOME ADULTS WILL BE
<u>VERY</u> UNCOMFORTABLE
ABOUT THIS BOOK. YOU'LL
SOON UNDERSTAND WHY.
IF AN ADULT IS READING
THIS TO YOU RIGHT NOW,
GIVE THEM A PAT ON THE
ARM AND TELL THEM IT
WILL BE <u>OK</u>. WRECKING
ISN'T ALWAYS A BAD
THING. BOOKS LIKE
TO BE READ AND USED
— THE MORE ACTIVELY
THE BETTER.

DIAL BOOKS FOR YOUNG READERS
AN IMPRINT OF PENGUIN RANDOM HOUSE LLC,
NEW YORK

FIRST PUBLISHED IN THE UNITED
STATES OF AMERICA BY DIAL BOOKS
FOR YOUNG READERS, AN IMPRINT
OF PENGUIN RANDOM HOUSE LLC, 2020

COPYRIGHT © 2020 BY KERI SMITH

VISIT US ONLINE AT PENGUINRANDOMHOUSE.COM.

LIBRARY OF CONGRESS CATALOGING-IN-
PUBLICATION DATA IS AVAILABLE.

PRINTED IN CHINA
ISBN 9780593111024

1 2 3 4 5 6 7 8 9 10

TEXT HAND-LETTERED BY KERI SMITH.

DESIGN BY KERI SMITH AND
JASON HENRY

THE ARTWORK FOR THIS BOOK WAS
CREATED WITH RECYCLED MATERIALS
INCLUDING CARDBOARD, CORK, WOOL,
NAILS, BITS OF FABRIC, OLD MAGAZINES,
STRING, DRINK LIDS, OLD BOOKS,
NEWSPAPERS, STICKS, TOILET PAPER ROLLS.

WRECK THIS PICTURE BOOK

KERI SMITH

DIAL BOOKS FOR YOUNG READERS

BLUMP.

THIS IS THE SOUND OF A BOOK SITTING.

IT IS JUST A LUMP ON A TABLE.

BORED.

IT DOESN'T HAVE ANYTHING TO DO.

IT IS SITTING AND
WAITING
FOR SOMEONE TO COME ALONG.

WHY DOES IT SIT
ALONE?

A LONG TIME AGO,
SOMEONE
(PROBABLY AN ADULT)
MADE UP SOME RULES
ABOUT BOOKS.

PROBABLY THIS
THIS
GUY
←

The Rules of Book Reading

1. Don't throw the book.

2. Don't fold the pages.

3. Don't be rough with the book.

4. Don't draw on the book.

5. Read quietly to yourself.

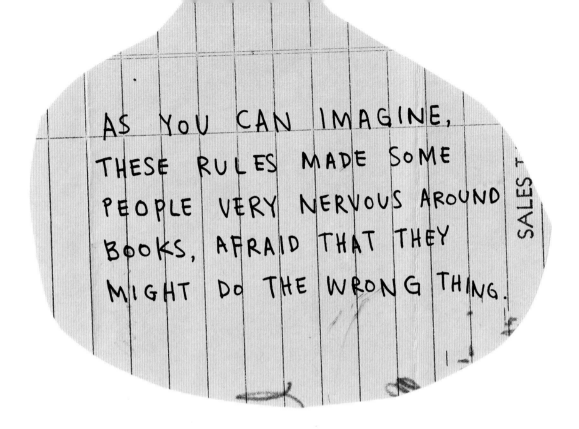

AS YOU CAN IMAGINE, THESE RULES MADE SOME PEOPLE VERY NERVOUS AROUND BOOKS, AFRAID THAT THEY MIGHT DO THE WRONG THING.

SALES

AND SO RATHER THAN RISK DOING THE WRONG THING, THEY MADE SURE TO DO AS LITTLE AS POSSIBLE WITH BOOKS.

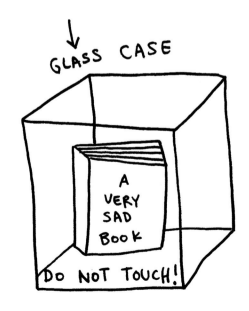

↓
GLASS CASE

A VERY SAD BOOK

DO NOT TOUCH!

IS A BOOK REALLY A BOOK IF IT ISN'T BEING USED?

WHAT IF I TOLD YOU THAT BOOKS
HAVE A SECRET WISH TO MOVE,
TO DANCE, TO GO ON ADVENTURES,
TO BE READ IN AS MANY WAYS AS
POSSIBLE?

EVERY BOOK HAS A WISH TO BE:

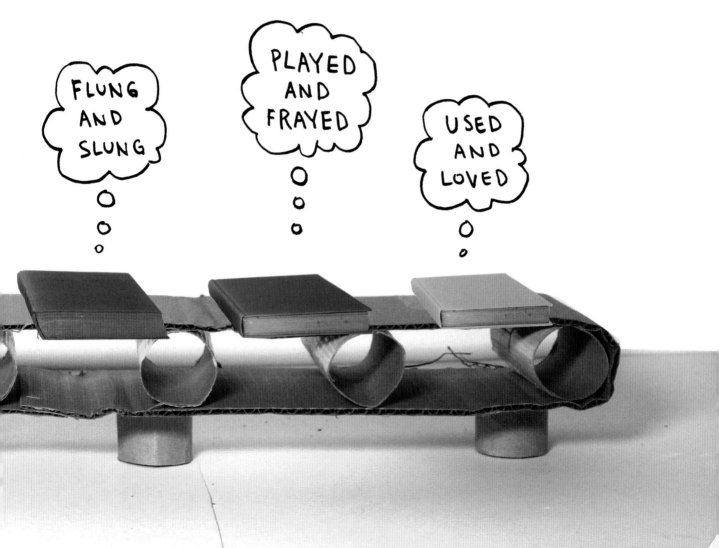

THANK GOODNESS YOU HAVE COME ALONG RIGHT AT THIS EXACT MOMENT! THE BOOK NEEDS YOU TO HELP MAKE ITS WISH COME TRUE!

DID YOU KNOW THAT A BOOK IS NOT ABLE TO BE ITSELF WITHOUT YOU? YOU HELP TO MAKE IT INTO SOMETHING. YOU BRING YOUR EXPERIENCES, YOUR IDEAS, AND YOUR IMAGINATION.

A BOOK CAN BE DIFFERENT EVERY TIME YOU READ IT BECAUSE _YOU_ CAN BE DIFFERENT (SILLY, HAPPY, SAD, QUIET).

SHAKE THIS WAY

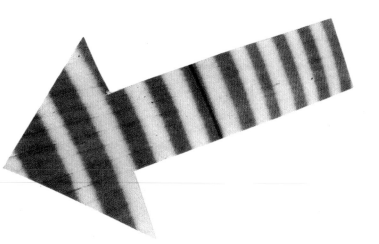

RUB YOUR
HANDS HERE

AND THAT WAY

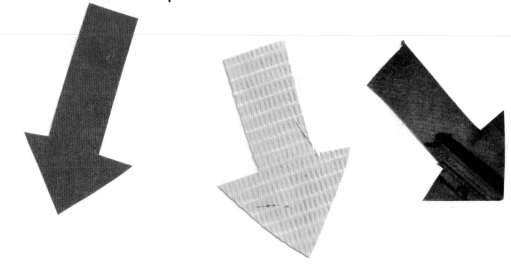

WHERE SHOULD WE **START**?

YOU MIGHT NEED TO SHAKE IT TO

WAKE IT UP.

NOW CLOSE YOUR EYES, AND
RUB YOUR HANDS ON THIS PAGE.

CAN YOU FEEL IT WAKING UP?
FASTER.

I THINK THIS IS WORKING.
YES!

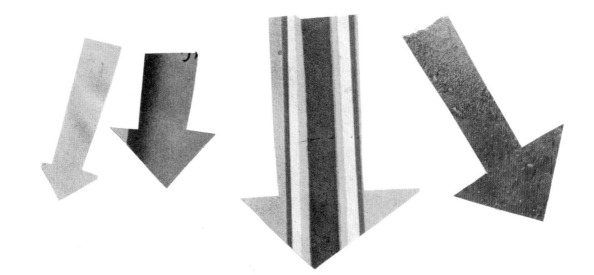

TOUCH THE PAGE AGAIN.
WHAT DOES IT FEEL LIKE?

TOUCH THE PAGE WITH YOUR FINGERS.
TOUCH THE PAGE WITH YOUR NOSE.
YOUR ELBOW.
HOW ABOUT YOUR TOES?

WHAT IF
YOU FOLD
DOWN SOME
CORNERS ?

TRY ROLLING
THIS PAGE UP.
YES !

YOU COULD DO SOME
FANCY FOLDS TO MAKE
THIS PAGE STAND UP
A LITTLE.

FOLD

Strato, thou hast been all
Farewell to thee too, Stra
My heart doth joy that y
I foun___ ___t he wa
I sh___ ___y this
Mor___ ___no e.
By ___ shal
So f ___ once
Hath ___d his h___
Night ha___ upon mine ey
That have but labour'd to

LOOK AT THE COLORS ON THIS PAGE. DID YOU KNOW THAT COLORS CAN VIBRATE? DOES IT LOOK LIKE THESE COLORS ARE MOVING? TRY BLINKING YOUR EYES. THIS CAN SHAKE THE BOOK A LITTLE.

NOW FLIP THE PAGES.

LISTEN TO THE SOUND THAT MAKES.

CAN YOU MAKE SOFT SOUNDS?

LITTLE SOUNDS?

FEATHERY SOUNDS?

THE SMALLEST SOUNDS IN THE UNIVERSE?

CAN YOU SQUINT YOUR EARS TO HEAR BETTER?

PRETEND YOU ARE THE WIND BLOWING THROUGH THE PAGES. BLOW ON THEM TO TURN THEM.

KNOCK HERE

HOW MANY DIFFERENT SOUNDS CAN YOU MAKE WITH THE BOOK?

TRY ALL OF THESE...

FLICK HERE

POKE HERE

BUMP YOUR ELBOW HERE

KNOCK HERE

SMELL THE BOOK.

WHAT DOES IT SMELL LIKE?

CAN READING MAKE YOU THINK
OF SMELLS?

COULD YOU ADD A SMELL TO THE
BOOK?

TAKE IT OUTSIDE. READ IT UNDER
A TREE, IN A SECRET HIDING SPOT,
WHILE YOU ARE ON AN ADVENTURE.

WHAT DOES IT SMELL LIKE WHERE
YOU ARE?

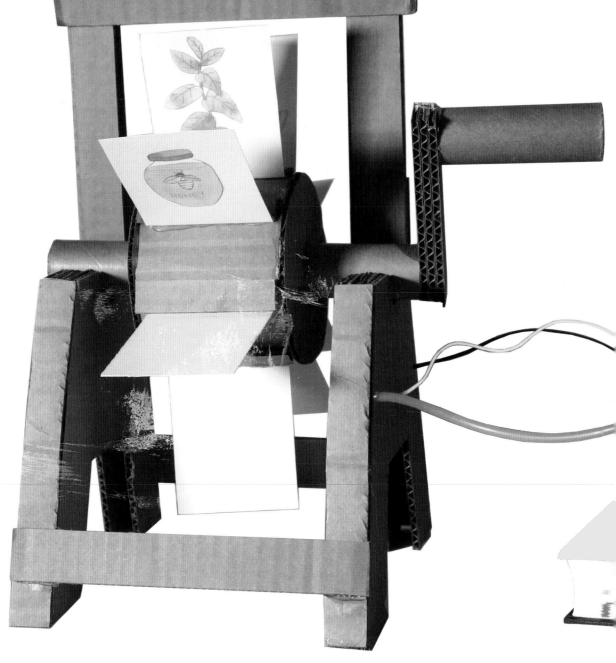

DO BOOKS HAVE A FLAVOR?
WHAT DO THEY TASTE LIKE?
COULD YOU ADD A FLAVOR?

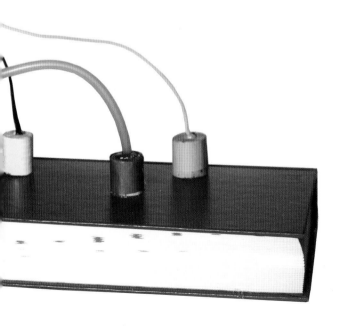

NOW THAT WE HAVE WOKEN
UP ALL OF OUR SENSES, HOW
ABOUT GOING ON SOME
ADVENTURES? THIS BOOK
SEEMS READY TO EXPLORE
NEW LANDS.

CAN YOU GIVE IT AN OUTFIT
OF SOME KIND?

MAYBE SOME SUNGLASSES
SO IT CAN SEE THINGS
BETTER IN THE DAYLIGHT?

THIS IS A BOOK JACKET

WHAT IF YOU COULD MAKE
THE BOOK FLY?
OH YES, NOW WE ARE
TALKING!

AH, EVERYBODY'S FAVORITE...

FIND A WAY TO WEAR THE BOOK.

(THIS BOOK LOVES TO GO WITH YOU EVERYWHERE.)

PLEASE NOTE:
THIS SPACE IS RESERVED FOR A PARTY.

Only dancing, singing, and general
merriment allowed.

WHAT IF YOU HAVE A PARTY FOR THE BOOK?

THIS IS ALSO A GOOD TIME FOR DANCING! BUMP, DROP, SPIN.

THE TOP SECRET SPY KIT

IF YOU FIND
THIS NOTE...
PLEASE LEAVE
A NOTE FOR
ME SOMEWHERE
IN THIS BOOK.

SECRET MESSAGE

HIDE A SECRET MESSAGE IN THE BOOK. SOMETHING YOU WANT THE NEXT READER TO KNOW.

I like reading books. They are amazing! I read them with mommy! mommy all day.

Jayne!
(age 5)

Hide the book in a secret spot that only you know about. Then go on a secret mission to find it.

PRETEND

YOU ARE

READING

THE BOOK

UPSIDE

DOWN.

WHAT IF YOU TIE A SCARF AROUND
IT AND MAKE IT INTO A PRESENT?
AND THEN CARRY IT AROUND
WITH YOU ALL DAY?
OR PRETEND IT IS A SECRET BOOK
THAT ONLY YOU CAN READ?

THIS BOOK CAN
BE ANYTHING.

WHAT IF YOU COULD REALLY MAKE THE
BOOK COME ALIVE? I JUST HAD AN
IDEA: IF YOU WANT SOMETHING TO
GROW, YOU PLANT A SEED. WHAT IF YOU
COULD TRY THAT? IT COULD BE AN
IMAGINARY SEED DRAWN BY YOU, OR
A REAL SEED.

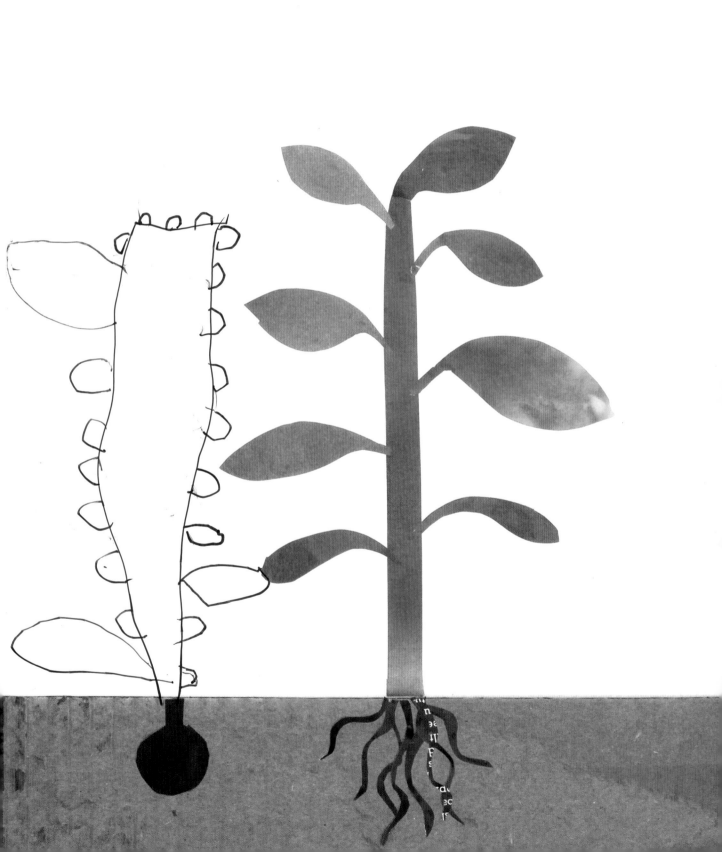

BE LIKE A ROCK TUMBLING DOWN
A HILL. ROLL WHILE HOLDING THE BOOK.
CAN YOU DO A SOMERSAULT?
CAN YOU ROLL THE BOOK BY ITSELF?

HOW DO YOU MAKE A BOOK RUN?

YOU CAN TELL A WELL-LOVED BOOK
BY HOW WRECKED IT IS.
HOW DOES THIS ONE LOOK NOW?
DO YOU KNOW THEY CALL A BOOK
THAT IS OLD-LOOKING
"DOG-EARED"?
IT USUALLY MEANS THAT THE EDGES
ARE WORN, THE COVER IS GRUBBY.

HOW DID YOU DO?

DOES THE BOOK
NEED TO REST?

YES

(TURN TO THE NEXT PAGE)

NO

(TURN TO THE FRONT OF THE
BOOK AND BEGIN AGAIN)

IT'S A NEW DAY.
SHALL WE BEGIN AGAIN?

WHAT WILL TODAY BRING FOR
YOU AND THE BOOK? IT LOOKS
LIKE YOU HAVE BECOME A REALLY
GOOD TEAM. AND THERE ARE
SO MANY WAYS TO SPEND TIME
WITH A BOOK...